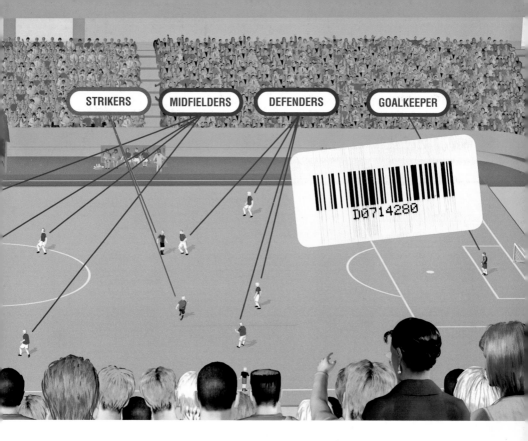

STRIKERS   MIDFIELDERS   DEFENDERS   GOALKEEPER

D0714280

This book will help you to understand what different players do for their teams, how they do it ... and where and why things can go horribly wrong.

You don't have to play football to be a spy. If you are a player, thinking about the games you watch will make you a better one. You can spy for fun or to help a team you support. It's up to you.

Next time you go to a game, or watch one on TV, do it the football spy way.

To all football spies

These spy notes tell you what to look out for when you're spying.

There are spy notes for the goalkeeper, defenders, midfielders and strikers.

What you need to do:

- Read the notes before the match. Look for the spy points.

- Watch the match.

- Give marks out of 10 for each part of the team. 10 is for ace and 0 is for hopeless.

- Add up the marks you have awarded to reach your spy **verdict** on the whole team.

Now go and do it!

Spy notes for the goalkeeper

What do goalkeepers do?

They stop goals from being scored. They have to be agile, acrobatic, quick off their line and brave.

What to look out for:

It helps if the goalkeeper is tall.
There are brilliant small goalkeepers, but they're at a disadvantage, and a football spy will always note this.

Good goalkeepers have the loudest voice on the field.

If they think a ball is theirs, they let their defenders know about it.

Watch out for silent goalkeepers.

Their defenders don't know whether or not they're coming for the ball. This is what can happen ... the spy will note this!

Good goalkeepers are decisive.

Watch out for goalkeepers who can't make up their minds.
They are often caught half in and half out of the goal.

Good goalkeepers make goalkeeping look simple.

They don't make easy saves look difficult.

Top goalkeepers can kick, throw and punch the ball well.
Accurate use of the ball by the goalkeeper at one end of the pitch
can lead to the chance of a goal at the other. A poor clearance can
put the goalkeeper's own goal in danger.

clearance: getting the ball away from the goal area

Even the best goalkeepers make mistakes.
Weak goalkeepers make them more often.
The spy notes when the goalkeeper loses
confidence after making a mistake.

Good goalkeepers don't make "lucky" saves.
Good goalkeepers get some part of their body, such as their
arm, leg or bottom, in the way of the **goalward** shot. This isn't
luck. It's the ability to react in a micro-second.

The 3 C's of goalkeeping.

Watch how the goalkeeper deals with high balls.

Look for the **3 C's**

1. Call

2. Come

3. Catch

The goalkeeper calls to tell the defenders to get out of the way, comes out of the goal area quickly, and catches the ball cleanly.

A good goalkeeper always deals with the ball at the highest point.

If the goalkeeper waits for the ball to arrive in his or her hands, a striker can cut across in front and reach the ball first.

A good goalkeeper punches balls they can't catch safely.

A goalkeeper who flaps at high balls is a poor goalkeeper!

Check all the things listed here. Now give your spy-marks out of 10 for the goalkeeper.

Spy notes for defenders

What do defenders do?

They defend their goal. Everything else they do is useless if they don't defend their goal properly.

What to look out for:

Defenders need to be fast.

A slow defender will often be beaten for speed by a quick attacker. The football spy never fails to spot this!

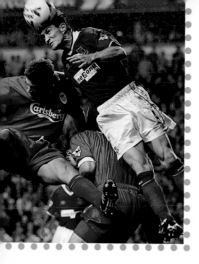

Defenders have to be able to head the ball well.

They head the ball.
The ball shouldn't
head them!

They need to be strong in the tackle.

14

A **tackle** from behind is a **foul**.

A two-footed tackle is a foul.

Defenders must pass accurately.

A spy will try to pick out the players who pass the ball well ... and those who don't!

A good pass from the defence often sets up a goal.

The moment when a team races forward in attack is often when they are at their weakest. A ball played quickly forward by a defender can lead to a goal against the attacking team – often against the run of play.

run of play: when one team appears to be playing better than the other

How defenders defend corners.

Corners are set pieces. Each team has its own way of defending them. In some teams each defender is given a player to mark at corners.

Other teams mark the spaces that players may move into, rather than the players themselves. This is called zonal marking.

Some teams place a player just inside each goalpost, to guard the goal.

A spy will check out whether the goalposts are guarded or not.

Key player

It helps if the spy can work out who is making the on-field decisions for the defence. There is usually a key player who does this.

You may see defenders arguing amongst themselves. This is often because they have a key player who isn't good at their job. This is just what a spy wants to know!

Good defenders work together.

They cover for each other. They don't yell in disgust when slow players keep being **outpaced** by the person they're marking. Instead, they try to help slower players. They might put in another player to mark the fast opponent or call a midfielder back to help the defender.

Good defenders learn to read the game.

What does that mean? It means spotting who is doing what in the other team, and trying to do something about it.

Watch out for the tall striker who always sets himself against the smallest defender. If the defence lets this happen, they're not reading the game.

Check all the things listed here. Now give your spy-marks out of 10 for the defence.

21

Spy notes for midfielders

What do midfielders do?

Everything! They defend, and attack. They create and score goals and stop the other team from doing either.

What to look out for:

Midfielders should control the midfield. The team that controls the midfield controls the game.

Midfielders should be able to run for ninety minutes.

A good spy will quickly spot a midfielder who tires easily.

There are different kinds of midfielders.

Holding midfielders will hold their defensive positions.

Attacking midfielders try to get forward into attack as often as they can. The sudden arrival of an attacking midfielder often leads to a goal.

Creative midfielders send short and long passes in every direction, creating chances for their team. The creative midfielder is often the most **influential** player in a team.

A football spy sees which players play in which way, and how good or bad they are at doing it.

24

Breaking up attacks.

Midfielders are at their most dangerous when they read an opponent's pass, and manage to cut it off, breaking up the attack as the other team is going forward.

Midfielders track back.

This means they follow attacking players on the other team, as they race through the defence hoping for a pass. If midfield tracking is poor, a team will probably lose.

Check all the things listed here. Now give your spy-marks out of 10 for the midfielders.

Spy notes for strikers

What do strikers do?

They score goals.

How a goal is scored doesn't matter. It can be a tap from a metre outside the goal, or a **free kick** from the halfway line. A goal is a goal, and goals win matches.

Strikers are attackers who play further up the pitch than the rest of the team. They can move to either side of the pitch to find space, but often they run down the centre of the pitch and strike for goal.

Is goal scoring all they do?

No. They try to make chances for their team-mates. It doesn't matter who scores, as long as someone scores.

What to look out for:

Some teams play with one striker, usually called a lone striker.

If a pass is played forward to the lone striker they either control the ball and play it to someone else or try to lose the defender who is marking them, and go for goal themselves. Lone strikers need strength on the ball. They have to be strong enough to keep the ball if they are tackled. They often use strength to win challenges in the **penalty** area.

Some teams play with two strikers.

Often one will be big and strong, the other small and quick.
The one with the ball will try to pass to a fellow striker.
The one without the ball will try to find a space to move into,
where they can receive a pass.

Some teams play with three strikers!

The third striker often plays just behind the front two,
hoping to nip in and score when they have confused
the defenders. This is called playing in the hole.

A defender can be a striker.

The football spy watches for defenders who run forward to attack. Usually defenders will run close to the **touchlines**, forcing the opposing defenders out of the centre.

Often defenders who do this will try to get beyond the other team's defence, running almost to the goal line. They either shoot ... **GOAL!** ... or pass the ball back to an **unmarked** attacker ... **GOAL!** ...

If attacking defenders are close enough to the other team's goal, they play a high ball across the penalty area, hoping that another player will get it ... **GOAL!**

Which defender does this?
Do they strike or pass?
That's what the football
spy wants to know.

31

The same is true for midfielders.

Sometimes midfielders will try to run into a space behind the defence. Sometimes they will run straight at the defence instead. If no one tackles them ... **GOAL!**

If they are tackled, they will often pass the ball just before the tackle is made, run past the tackler and receive the ball back ... **GOAL!**

The football spy takes careful note of players who do this, and whether they do it well.

Often the most dangerous striker is the free kick ace.

What do free kick aces do?

They take free kicks, corners and penalties. It is how they take them that matters. They can swerve the ball, like this ... **GOAL!**

They can go for power, like this ... **GOAL!**

A free kick ace may be on the **team sheet** as a midfielder or
defender. Don't be fooled by this.

Goals are their business.

Free kick aces have football brains. Often, when they are expected to shoot, they play a clever pass instead. Like this ... **GOAL!**

The football spy watches free kick aces very carefully, checking the methods they like to use and how good they are at it.

Now award spy-marks out of 10 for the strikers!

Spy verdict

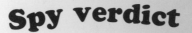

Now it's time to give your spy verdict on the team you've been watching.

Take the scores you've written down for each part of the team, and add them together to give your final spy verdict!

It is simple to do, but it works. Good luck ... and good spying!

Understanding your scores

0–10   This team is terrible. There is lots of room for improvement.

11–25   This team is fairly average. They're not likely to have high goal scores.

26–35   This team is good, with plenty of goals and teamwork between the players.

36–40   This is the perfect team. They're hard to beat!

Glossary

corners   free kicks from the corners of the field.

foul   to break the rules of a game by playing dangerously.

free kicks   free kicks are direct or indirect. A direct free kick can be kicked directly in the opponent's goal. When an indirect free kick is taken, the ball must touch another player before it enters the goal.

goalward   heading towards the goal

influential   making a difference

outpaced   to be overtaken by someone who is faster

penalty   if a foul is committed on an attacking player within the opposing penalty area, the attacking team has one free shot at the goal from the penalty spot.

tackle   to try to get the ball from a player on the opposite team

team sheet   a list of the names of the players in each team and the position they'll be playing in for the game

touchlines   the two longer sidelines of a pitch

unmarked   a player who does not have another player from the opposing team, trying to make it difficult for them to receive a pass.

verdict   final opinion

Index

⦾ Ideas for guided reading ⦾

Learning objectives: locate information; compare the way that information is presented in different texts (screen and print-based); read information texts and identify main points; explain a process and present information effectively to an audience

Curriculum links: PE: Invasion games (1)

Interest words: goalkeeper, defender, midfielder, striker, spy verdict, decisive, clearance, set pieces, zonal marking, influential, opponent, free kick ace, penalties

Resources: small whiteboards, football magazines, a recording of a football match

Getting started

This book can be read over two or more guided reading sessions.

- Ask the children what a spy does. Can they think of any famous spies? (James Bond) Explain that the book is called *Football Spy* and ask the children what they think this is.
- Read the front and back covers together. Ask the children to discuss what the book may tell them about football.
- Ask the children: *What makes a winning football team? What makes a losing team?*
- Ask them to list some qualities of top professional football players and their teams.

Reading and responding

- Walk through the book and then read pp2-3 together. Model how to use the punctuation to read and make sense of the sentences.
- Ask the children to explain what a football spy does. Check that they understand that they don't have to be football players to be a spy.
- Look at the picture on pp2-3 and identify some of the players in the team (*goalkeepers, defenders, strikers, midfielders*).
- Return to the contents and ask them to choose spy notes for a certain player, and read them in pairs.